Dear Junior Gymnast:

Hi! I'm Dominique Dawes, I've been tumbling, twisting, and flipping since I was six years old.

I would always go straight to the gym after school. Since I spent so much time there, most of my friends were gymnasts. They understood what it was like to spend so many hours practicing a sport you love.

But I had friends from school who didn't do gymnastics. Sometimes they would get upset when I couldn't hang out in the afternoons or join after-school clubs with them. But they would always come to my meets and cheer me on.

In this book Dana Lewis has a friend problem, too — when her gymnastics schedule is about to ruin her best friend's birthday! What will she do? Let's find out!

Dominique Dawes

Read more books about the Junior Gymnasts!

Dana's Best Friend

JUNIOR GYMNASTS

Dana's Best Friend

BY TEDDY SLATER

illustrated by Wayne Alfano

A
LITTLE APPLE
PAPERBACK

SCHOLASTIC INC.
New York Toronto London Auckland Sydney

With special thanks to
Tom Manganiello of the
57th Street Magic Gym.

A PARACHUTE PRESS BOOK

ISBN 0-590-86003-8

12 11 10 9 8 7 6 5   8 9/9 0 1/0

Printed in the U.S.A.   40

First Scholastic printing, September 1996

For Judith Kiersky

Contents

Dana's Best Friend

1
Double Trouble

"Last year it was a circus party," I told Amanda Calloway. "And the year before that it was a skating party. There's always a theme, and it's always something different."

"Dana and Becky have the best birthday parties in Springfield!" Katie Magee declared.

It was Monday afternoon at Jody's Gym. Katie, Amanda, and I were in the locker room getting ready for class. And we were talking about the super-amazing birthday party my best friend, Becky Berkman, and I have every year.

I'm Dana Lewis, and I'm nine years, eleven months, and seventeen days old. A week from this Sunday I'll be ten! Katie is only eight and a half, and Amanda is nine and a half. But we're all on the same Level 5 gymnastics team. Katie and I have been taking lessons at Jody's Gym since we were little, but Amanda just joined a few months ago when she moved here from Chicago.

"How come you and Becky don't have your own parties?" Amanda asked me.

"Becky and Dana do everything together," Katie chimed in.

"Becky's mom and my mom met when they were both pregnant," I explained. "I was born exactly one week after Becky, and we've been best friends ever since!"

"Wow!" said Amanda, stepping into her bright pink leotard. "You're almost twins."

"My dad calls us the Un-twins!" I giggled. "He also calls us Double Trouble!"

Katie pulled a black leotard out of her gym bag. "I wish I had a twin," she said. Katie is an only child. Her parents got divorced last year, so now she lives with just her mother.

"I don't!" Amanda exclaimed. "My family's big enough already."

I nodded. Amanda's family is huge! Besides her mother and father, she has two sisters, one brother, one grandmother, and seven pets in her house!

Amanda smiled at Katie. "At least you don't have to share everything," she said. "You're lucky!"

I think *I'm* the one who's really lucky. My family isn't too big or too small. It's just right. There's me, my mom, my dad, my little brother, Freddy, and our dog, Woof.

When we were all dressed for gym,

Katie, Amanda, and I went to the mirror to fix our hair. Coach Jody makes us pull it back for practice. She says gymnastics is hard enough when you can see — and it's really hard looking through your hair!

Hannah Rose Crenshaw, Liz Halsey, and Emily Stone were already in front of the mirror. Those are the other girls on our team. They've been coming to my birthday parties for years. They moved over to make room for us.

"You guys are late," Hannah Rose said, pinning her hair into a bun. Sometimes Hannah Rose acts as if she is our boss. But I like her anyway.

Amanda wound a bright pink ribbon through her thick brown braid. It was the exact same color as her leotard, and it looked great with her dark skin and eyes. Katie's blond hair was already up in pigtails.

She gave them a tug while I squished my curly red mop through a ponytail clip.

"How come Becky doesn't do gymnastics?" Amanda asked.

"She used to," Katie explained. "But now she's into karate."

"Becky can do everything!" I told Amanda. "She already knows how to tap dance, juggle, and play the trumpet."

"She sounds cool," Amanda said.

"Becky is super-cool!" I agreed. Amanda has met Becky only a couple of times, so she doesn't know her very well. Becky and I both go to Lincoln Elementary School. But Katie and Amanda live closer to Washington Elementary, so they go to school there.

"So what kind of party are you having this year?" Amanda asked me.

"A karate party!" I said. "It's going to be at Becky's *dojo*."

Hannah Rose made a face. "Becky's *what*?" she asked.

"Her *dojo*," I repeated. "That's what you call a karate school in Japanese. Her teacher is going to show us how to do karate chops. We might learn how to break bricks with our bare hands!"

"Really?" Liz gasped.

"Sure," I said. "And Becky's mom is getting a special kind of cake, and Becky and I are making this great piñata, and — "

"What's a piñata?" Amanda interrupted.

"It's a big papier-mâché thing filled with candy," I told her. "Everyone gets blindfolded and hits it with sticks until it breaks. Then all the goodies fall out."

"Yum!" Amanda said. "That sounds like fun."

"It is," Katie said. "Dana and Becky make a new piñata every year. It's always shaped like some kind of animal."

"I can't wait for your party," Amanda told me.

"I can't either!" I said. "It's going to be terrific!"

"What are we supposed to wear?" Hannah Rose asked. "I don't have any karate clothes."

"I don't either," I said. "I'm going to wear my leotard and tights."

"I guess I'll wear a leo, too," Amanda decided.

"A red one!" we all said together. Amanda is totally superstitious. She has a different lucky color for every day of the week. Sunday is her red day.

"What are the rest of you guys wearing?" I asked.

Before anyone could answer, Katie yelled, "Hey! It's almost three-thirty."

"We'd better go," Hannah Rose told us. "You know how Coach Jody gets when we're late for warm-up."

But when we ran into the gym, Coach Jody hardly even glanced at us. She was busy talking with Lila Hanks.

Lila is the best gymnast on the Elite team. That's the best team at Jody's Gym. Most of the Elites are teenagers. They get to compete in all the big meets. Everyone on my team loves Lila.

As we took our places on the mats, Coach Jody whispered something in Lila's ear. She had to bend down to do it. Way down. Coach Jody is over six feet tall!

After a minute Coach Jody glanced up and smiled at us. "I have a very special announcement to make," she said. "Someone from our gym has been invited to the U.S. National Championships!" She gave Lila a big smile.

"I guess you know who I'm talking about," Coach Jody said as we all let out a cheer.

"Hold on, girls," Coach Jody said. "That's not all. In two weeks Lila will be going to Texas to train with Olympic Coach Jon Sokolov. Before she leaves, she's agreed to give a special exhibition for all the other gymnasts who work out here. After that, *we're* going to give *her* something — a big farewell party in the gym!"

Everyone cheered again.

Coach Jody held up her hand. "There's more," she said. "A TV crew from Channel Four will be here to tape the whole thing. They want to run a special piece about Lila on the local news — 'A Day in the Life of a National Gymnast.' "

"Yippee!" Katie cried. "Maybe I'll get to be on TV!"

"Me, too!" I said. "I bet we — "

"Don't be silly," Hannah Rose butted in. "Lila's the one who's going to the Nationals. Not us."

Hannah Rose can be a real party pooper. But I didn't care. I had a feeling we were *all* going to be on TV. Wow!

"So tell your parents about it tonight," Coach Jody said. "The big day is Sunday. And you're all invited."

Everyone started talking at once.

"Did Coach Jody say Sunday?" I asked Katie. "*This* Sunday?"

"Uh-huh," Katie answered.

"Oh, no!" I gasped. "It *can't* be Sunday. That's the day of Becky's and my birthday party!"

2

The Flower Aunts

As soon as practice ended, I ran to the locker room and changed back into my school clothes. I was already dressed when the other girls came in.

Katie plopped right down on the floor and pulled her diary out of her gym bag.

"What are you doing?" I asked.

"I want to write down everything Coach Jody said about Lila," Katie said. Katie likes to write down everything about everything! She never goes anywhere without her diary. Usually I think that's pretty cool. But today I was in a rush.

"Where are you going?" Katie asked as I put on my jacket. "Aren't you going to wait for Amanda and me?"

I looked around for Amanda. She was standing in front of the mirror, stretching out.

"I can't," I said. "I've got to go tell Becky about Lila's party. We have to change *our* party to some other day."

"Dana!" Mrs. Berkman cried when I rang Becky's bell a little while later. "You're just the person we need around here. Becky's having a clothes crisis."

"A clothes crisis?" I repeated. "Since when does Becky care about clothes?"

"She doesn't," Mrs. Berkman said. "But I do!"

"Oh," I said. "I didn't know you cared either."

Mrs. Berkman laughed. "Actually, I don't," she admitted. "But my sister Violet is in town. We're all having dinner at that fancy French restaurant on River Road. The whole family is going — Rose and Lily and Pansy, too."

"You left out Iris," I reminded her. Mrs. Berkman and her sisters all have flower names. Hers is Daisy. Becky and I call them the Flower Aunts.

"Oops!" Mrs. Berkman said. "Can't forget Iris! Anyway, since you know Becky's whole family *and* her whole wardrobe, maybe you can help her find something to wear."

"No problem," I said, heading up the stairs to Becky's room.

Becky's door was open, but I could hardly get inside. There were piles of clothing all over the floor. For someone who doesn't care about clothes, Becky has an awful lot of them.

I stepped over a stack of sweaters and found Becky lying on her bed in a pair of white pajamas. Her short black hair was sticking out all over.

"Hi, Beck," I said. "Your mom said you were having a clothes crisis. How come you're wearing pajamas?"

Becky jumped off the bed and smoothed down her hair. "I'm not wearing pj's," she explained. "This is my karate outfit — my *gi*! Do you like it?"

"I love it!" I said. "You look totally cool."

"Mom won't let me wear it to dinner," Becky complained. "She says the aunts wouldn't approve."

I like Becky's aunts. They're all very nice. But sometimes they can be kind of stuffy. It's hard to believe Becky's mom comes from the same family. Mrs. Berkman isn't stuffy at all. She's really fun — just like Becky!

"Come on," I told Becky. "I'll help you find something else to wear."

Becky plopped down next to the sweaters. "I don't see why I have to get all dressed up for my aunts. They already know what I look like."

"Why don't you wear your navy jumper?" I suggested.

"Way too boring!" Becky said. "Even for the aunts."

"The shiny blouse and black skirt?" I tried again.

"*Bor*-ing!" Becky picked up a fuzzy pink dress and put it down again. "This looks like a little kid's party dress," she muttered.

"Party dress!" I yelped. "Oh, my gosh! I almost forgot! The *party*! The reason I came over is we have to change the date of our party."

"Change it?" Becky asked. "What are you talking about?"

"Lila Hanks is going to be in the

National Gymnastics Championships!" I announced.

Becky held a sparkly T-shirt up against her shoulders. "You're kidding!" she said.

"Nope." I tossed the T-shirt back on the pile. "Coach Jody just told us about it at practice."

"Wow!" Becky cried. "That's awesome. But what does it have to do with our party?"

"Lila is going to do a special exhibition for everyone at the gym — this Sunday!" I said. "After that we're having a big party for her. And the whole thing is going to be on TV!"

"You're kidding!" Becky said again.

I bounced on Becky's bed. "A camera crew from Channel Four is coming. They're doing a show about Lila, and my whole team might get to be in it!"

"That's fantastic!" Becky said.

"I know!" I agreed. "Except for the Sunday part."

"Oh, right!" Becky said. "Well, can't they change the day so you can go, too?"

"Nope. It's all arranged," I explained. "So we have to change *our* party."

"But *our* party is all arranged, too," Becky said. "And this year it's even on my real birthday! I don't *want* to change it."

"Come on, Becky," I said. "I *can't* miss Lila's exhibition. Going to the Nationals is a really big deal."

"I know that," Becky said. "But it's not like *you're* going."

"Please, Beck!" I cried. "This is really important!"

"Well, my birthday's important, too!" Becky argued.

"Please, Becky!" I begged. "Please, please, please, please, please — "

"Okay! Okay!" Becky laughed. "You sound like your little brother! I'll ask my mom to call the karate center. Maybe we can change our party to Saturday."

"Thanks, Becky," I said. "I knew you'd understand!"

Becky grinned. "You're welcome." And then she said, "I have a better idea. As long as we're changing the party, let's make it next Sunday. If we can't have it on *my* birthday, we might as well have it on *yours*."

"Great!" I said. "When it comes to best friends, you are the very best!"

"I know!" Becky said. "Now help me find something to wear."

"Sure," I said. Then I reached into her closet and pulled out a bright blue dress. It had big yellow sunflowers all around the bottom. "Here, try this."

Becky took the dress with one hand and high-fived me with the other. "It's perfect!" she said. "The Flower Aunts will love it."

3
Triple Trouble

"It's all set," I announced Wednesday afternoon. "Becky and I are having our party *next* Sunday — on my real birthday!"

"Great," Amanda said. "Then we can all go to Lila's party *and* to yours!"

It was 5:30 and practice was over, but Amanda, Katie, and I didn't feel like leaving yet.

Hannah Rose, Liz, and Emily disappeared into the locker room. Katie bounced on the trampoline.

"I'm going to stay here and practice some more," Amanda said. "I want to look

21

good for the TV cameras on Sunday."

"Coach Jody didn't say *we* were definitely going to be on TV," Katie pointed out. "The cameras will be there for Lila."

"I bet they'd show us, too, if we did something really special," I said.

"Like what?" Katie asked.

"I don't know." I shrugged my shoulders and kicked up into a handstand. I do my best thinking that way. Upside down! It must have something to do with all the blood rushing to my head.

I was just starting to get dizzy when I figured it out. I flopped down on the mat.

"What if we worked out a whole routine on the trampoline?" I suggested. "Something we could all do together."

"That's a good idea!" Katie said. "*Triple* trouble! The TV guys would definitely notice that."

"It's a *great* idea," Amanda declared. "Let's do it!"

But before we could start, the gym door banged opened and Becky burst in.

"HAAIII-*yaa!*" she yelled, striking a karate pose. "Hi, Dana! Hi, Katie! Hi, Amanda!"

"HI, BECKY," we all yelled back. Sometimes it's hard to talk in a normal voice when Becky is around.

"What are *you* doing here?" I asked.

"I can't stay," Becky said. "My mom's waiting outside in the car. But I have to tell you something, Dana."

"What is it?" I asked.

But Becky just stood there.

"What?" I repeated.

Katie looked from Becky to me and back again. Then she grabbed Amanda's sleeve and pulled her over to the other side of the trampoline.

As soon as we were alone, Becky said, "I made my mom stop here on the way

home from karate so I could tell you some-thing."

"What?" I asked for the third time.

Becky paused again. Then she said, "Listen, Dana. My mom tried to change the day of our party, but the *dojo* is booked up till next month, so we can't! The party has to be *this* Sunday."

"But Sunday is *Lila's* party!" I wailed. "I'm supposed to go there! Now what am I going to do?"

"You're going to come to the karate party," Becky said. "You have to! Everything is all set. My mom already ordered the cake. Besides, it's your party, too. Right?"

There was a long silence. I didn't know what to say.

"Dana?" Becky said.

"Uh-huh," I mumbled.

"You *have* to come," Becky repeated. She looked really upset.

"But no one from my gym will be there," I argued. "They're all going to Lila's exhibition. How can it be my party without my friends?"

There was another silence. I glanced over the trampoline. Katie and Amanda were just standing there, watching us.

"I have an idea," Becky suddenly exclaimed. "You can come to my party on Sunday and then have your own party at the gym *next* Sunday. That way your other friends will be able to come, too."

"But — " I started to say.

"We'll have two parties!" Becky went on. "And they'll both be on our actual birthdays!"

"What about our birthday candles?" I asked. "We always blow them out together."

"We can still do that," Becky said. "But we'll have two cakes, so we'll get to do it twice! You can help blow mine out at my party and I'll help blow yours out at *your* party."

"Well," I said, "if you — "

"You'll see," Becky insisted. "It will be great!" All of a sudden she seemed really excited. But now *I* felt awful. Becky still didn't understand how important Lila's exhibition was.

Before I could say anything else, a car honked outside. "That's my mom," Becky said. "I have to go!" Then she yelled good-bye to Katie and Amanda and ran out the door.

After Becky left, I plopped down on the edge of the trampoline.

"What's going on?" Amanda asked. "Is Becky really having a party the same day as Lila's exhibition?"

"Uh-huh," I said. "And I just said I would go to *Becky's* party instead of Lila's. I can't believe I did that!"

Katie patted my arm. "I wish you could come to Lila's party with us," she said. "But you did the right thing. Didn't she, Amanda?"

"No way!" Amanda exclaimed. "Birthdays happen every year. Dana's already had nine of them! But how often does someone we know get to go to the Nationals? I think you should call Becky when you get home," she said to me. "Just tell her you changed your mind."

"I can't!" I cried. "Becky's my best friend! I *have* to go to her party . . . don't I?"

4
Becky's Birthday

"Do you want a ride to Becky's party?" my mother asked me Sunday afternoon.

"That's okay, Mom," I said, putting my warm-up suit on over my leotard. "The *dojo* is only a few blocks past the gym. I can bike there."

"Well, ride safely," she said. "And wish Becky a happy birthday for me."

"I will," I promised.

I just hope Becky appreciates this! I thought as I wheeled my bicycle out of the garage.

I was still mad about missing Lila's exhibition. But as I pedaled off to Becky's party, I let out a few karate yells — just to get in the mood.

"*Haaaiii*-yaa!" I yelled. "Haaaiii-*yaa!*" And finally *"HAAAIII-YAA!"*

"Hi, yourself!" yelled a little boy on Rollerblades.

I turned left on Cranberry Street and kept going. After a while I came to Jody's Gym. The parking lot was full of cars. As I rode past, I spotted a big white van with CHANNEL 4 NEWS written in black letters on the side.

I slowed down and turned my bike around. I stared at the truck. Maybe I'll just look in the window, I thought. I've never seen a real TV camera before.

I climbed off my bike and put it in the bike rack. Then I ran over to the van. It would only take a minute to look at the cameras.

"Dana?" someone called.

It was Katie. She and Amanda were just getting out of Katie's mom's car. They both ran over to me.

"Dana! What are *you* doing here?" Amanda asked. "We thought you were going to *Becky's* party."

"I'm on my way there," I answered. "I just stopped to look at the TV cameras."

Amanda stood up on her tiptoes and peeked inside the van. "It's empty!" she announced.

"They must have taken everything into the gym," Katie said.

"Rats!" I grumbled. "I wanted to see."

"Then come inside with us," Amanda suggested.

"I'd better not," I said. "Becky's party starts at two o'clock. It's almost two now."

"This will only take a minute," Katie urged. "Besides, don't you want to wish Lila good luck?"

"Well . . ." I said. "Okay. But just for a minute." I followed my friends into the gym.

"Yikes!" Katie squealed when we were all inside. "Look at all these people! I wonder where Lila is."

"I don't see her," Amanda said.

I glanced around the room. All I could see were a million legs. There were a lot of grown-ups in the room. Tall ones!

"She has to be here somewhere," I said.

I took my backpack off and handed it to Katie. Then I climbed up on the balance beam so I could see over everyone.

"There!" I pointed to the vaulting horse on the other side of the gym. Lila and Coach Jody were leaning against it. A man in a blue blazer stuck a microphone in front of their faces.

Liz and Hannah Rose stood next to them. I could tell Hannah Rose was trying to get in front of the camera.

Katie and Amanda started squeezing through the crowd. I hopped back down and squeezed after them. I'll just say hi to Lila, I decided. Then I'll leave.

It took forever to get across the room to our teammates. By then, Lila was already doing her floor exercise.

"Looking good, Lila!" a man with a big camera on his shoulder yelled out. Everyone else was being really quiet.

It was boiling hot under the TV lights. Katie and Amanda took off their warm-up suits.

"I'd better go," I whispered to them.

"You might as well wait till she's done," Katie whispered back. "Her whole routine is only two and a half minutes."

"I guess I can stay for two and a half minutes," I agreed. I took off my warm-ups, too.

I thought Lila looked nervous, and I

guess she was. She finished her first tumbling run flat on her bottom!

"Can we try that again?" asked a woman holding a clipboard and stopwatch.

Lila did it again without falling, but she was kind of wobbly. The TV people didn't seem to notice. This time, *Lila* asked to do it again. "I know I can do better," she said.

Lila's third try wasn't just better. It was perfect! Everybody clapped. They were still clapping when the clipboard lady said, "Sorry, Lila. I'm afraid you'll have to do it one more time. You were great, but we ran out of tape."

"No problem!" Lila said. But there *was* a problem. The next time she tried, she fell again.

I looked up at the clock. It was 2:15. "I have to go," I told Katie and Amanda. "I'm already late for Becky's party."

"You can't go now," Amanda said. "You'll jinx Lila."

"Oh, A-*man*-da," I groaned. "You are so superstitious!" But I didn't think it would hurt to stay another two and a half minutes. Just in case.

Lila and the TV people finally got it right — on the sixth try!

"Now I've *got* to go," I told my friends.

I was heading toward the door when Coach Jody blew her whistle. Everyone stopped what they were doing.

"Ladies and gentlemen!" Coach Jody began. "As you know, Channel Four is here to film a day in the life of our very own champion — Lila Hanks!"

Coach Jody paused as we all cheered. "On a normal day, there would be gymnasts working out," she went on. "So they want some background shots of our younger gymnasts. I'm going to ask the Level Five and Six girls to pretend this is just a regular day at the gym. If the rest of you would please move to the side, I think we'll be fine."

As everyone moved back, Katie and Amanda moved forward — toward Coach Jody. I stayed where I was.

"Come on, Dana," Katie said. "Don't you want to be on TV?"

"Of course she does," Amanda answered. "You can do just a couple of vaults," she told me. "That won't take long."

"I'll spot you," Katie said. "Then we can *both* get on TV!"

"I really don't think I should," I said.

"Well, *I'm* going to do my balance beam routine," Amanda announced. "That's my best event."

"Hey!" Hannah Rose cried. "*I* want to do the beam routine!" She raced after Amanda.

Katie moved to the horse. "Are you ready, Dana?" she asked.

I took a deep breath. "Ready," I said. Then I ran down the runway, bounced off the springboard, and went vaulting over the horse.

"Yay, Dana!" Katie cheered after I nailed the landing.

A lot of other people clapped for me. It was a pretty good vault, if I say so myself!

"Hey, check out the little redhead," the woman with the clipboard told the cameraman. "Let's get a shot of her."

"Sure," the cameraman said, pointing his camera at me. "Let's see you do that again," he said.

So I gave him a big smile and did it again.

And again.

And again.

After a while, I started getting tired. But I didn't mind. I was definitely going to be on TV!

About the millionth time I did it, the

clipboard lady finally said, "Perfect! That's a wrap!"

Katie hurried over with Liz and Emily. Amanda ran over, too. Hannah Rose was still on the beam.

"Hey, Dana!" Amanda said. "You were awesome!"

"Super-awesome!" Katie cried.

"Good going, kiddo," Coach Jody said. "That last vault was the best I've ever seen you do. It's going to look great on TV!"

I was still trying to catch my breath, so I didn't answer. I just grinned.

"I bet you worked up an appetite with all those vaults," Coach Jody said with a smile. "Why don't you have a bite to eat?"

"Yeah, you should see the food table!" Emily said. She pointed toward the back of the gym. A long table had been set up against the wall. But you could hardly see the table because there were so many trays of food on it.

My friends all ran toward the table, so I followed them.

"Wow!" Katie cried, reaching for a tiny little hot dog. "Look at all this stuff."

I took a hot dog, too. It had a blue plastic toothpick stuck through the middle.

The minute I popped the hot dog into my mouth, Amanda said, "This is the best party I've ever been to. Now aren't you glad you stayed, Dana?"

"Stayed?" I repeated. "Oh, no! I didn't mean to *stay* here! I meant to go to *Becky's* party!"

I spit my hot dog into a napkin and raced from the gym. Becky's going to kill me! I thought. And I couldn't even blame her. I felt like the worst best friend in the world!

The Fight

I hopped on my bike and rode off as fast as I could. Maybe it wasn't too late. Maybe if I hurried, I could still make it to Becky's party.

But when I got to the *dojo,* I didn't see the Berkmans' car out front. I didn't see *any* cars! "Uh-oh," I said.

I leaned my bike against the fence and ran inside anyway. The karate center was empty. There wasn't even anyone in the office. The big clock on the wall said 4:25.

Suddenly I heard a strange swishing sound. Maybe that's the party! I thought. I followed the sound down the hall to a big room with mirrors on the walls. The shiny wood floor was covered with confetti, jelly beans, and pieces of piñata. Two men in overalls were sweeping it up with gigantic brooms.

"Hi," I said. They stopped sweeping.

"Looking for someone?" the first man asked.

"Becky Berkman," I replied. "I'm looking for her birthday party."

"Well, you found the place," the other man said. "But the party's over. The birthday girl and her parents left a few minutes ago. You just missed them."

"Yup," the first man agreed. "The party's over."

I couldn't believe it. I had missed my best friend's birthday.

As soon as I rang Becky's doorbell, Mrs. Berkman threw open the door.

"Dana!" she cried. "Where have you been? We were worried sick!"

Then she hugged me so tight I couldn't talk. I could hardly breathe.

"Becky!" Mrs. Berkman yelled, pulling me inside. "Look who's here."

A second later Becky appeared. "Are you okay?" she asked. "What happened? We thought you got run over or kidnapped or something."

"I'm sorry, Beck," I said. "I can't believe I missed your party. I was on my way there when — "

"Wait a sec," Becky broke in. "You'd better call your mom. She kind of freaked out when she heard you were missing."

"Missing!" I said. "Who told her I was missing?"

"I did," Becky said. "When you weren't at the *dojo* by two-thirty, I called your house. Your mom said you'd left half an hour ago!"

"Oh, no!" I groaned. "She must be going crazy by now."

"Well . . . she was pretty upset the last time she called," Becky said.

"The *last* time?" I gulped. "How many times did she call?"

"She's been calling every fifteen minutes," Becky said. "First at the *dojo* and then here."

Uh-oh, I thought. Now I'm going to get it! I reached for the hall telephone.

My mother picked up on the first ring. "Dana?" she screamed into the phone. "Is that you?"

"Yes, it's me, Mom."

"Oh, Dana, honey," she cried. "Thank goodness. Are you all right? Where are you? Where *were* you? What happened?"

"I'm fine," I said. "I'm at the Berkmans' now. And nothing happened. I — "

"Then why weren't you at Becky's party?" she interrupted me.

"I was on my way there . . ." I began.

"And?" my mother prompted. Now she sounded annoyed, but at least she wasn't screaming anymore.

"Well, I had to pass the gym on the way," I said. "So I thought I'd stop in for just a minute to see what was going on."

"And?" my mother said again.

"When I got there, Lila was getting ready to do her floor routine," I explained. "It only lasts for two and a half minutes, so I thought it would be okay to stay and watch."

I stopped talking as Mrs. Berkman tugged on my ponytail. I looked up, and she smiled.

"I'm so glad you're okay, Dana," she said. Then she went into the kitchen.

"Dana?" my mom's angry voice came over the phone. "Are you still there?"

"Sorry, Mom," I said. "Mrs. Berkman just left." I rolled my eyes at Becky. She was

45

standing right near the phone, listening.

"Anyway," I went on, "some people from the TV station were videotaping Lila's routine. They wanted it to be perfect, so she had to keep doing it over and over. They kept stopping her in the middle."

"Even so," my mother said, "it couldn't have taken all day."

"Well, then the TV people wanted us to pretend we were having a normal practice session," I continued. "So I did a vault. And a guy with a camera started shooting me. And guess what! He says I'm going to be on TV tonight! On the six o'clock news! Isn't that incredible?"

There was a long silence on the other end of the phone. I waited for my mom to say something.

"Yes, that's incredible," she finally said. "It's incredible that you didn't even think to call me or Becky and let us know where you were. Do you have any idea how worried everyone was?"

But before I could answer, she said, "I thought you knew better, Dana. Now I want you to come right home. We'll talk more about this later."

"I'm sorry, Mom," I said. "I didn't think you'd worry." But it was too late. She'd already hung up the phone.

"I have to go," I told Becky. "My mom's really mad. Besides, I want to get home before the news comes on."

I raised my hand for a high five, but Becky just looked at it.

"What's the matter?" I asked. "You don't seem very excited. Don't you want to hear about me on TV?"

"Why should I?" Becky said. "You didn't even ask about my party."

"Oh, no! Your party!" I cried. I had forgotten all about it! "How was it?"

"It was awful!" Becky exclaimed. waited and waited for you to show up. Half the kids went home before we finally broke the piñata and brought out the cake. And then I had to blow out the candles all by myself. You ruined my whole party!"

"Oh no," I said. "I'm really sorry. I didn't mean to stay at the gym — I was just so excited about being on TV. I can't believe I missed your party."

Becky's eyes filled with tears. "I can't either," she said. "I can't believe you skipped *my* party and went to *Lila's*. Best friends don't act that way."

"But I *said* I'm sorry," I repeated. "And I am!"

"Well, I'm sorry, too," Becky said. "I'm sorry you're not my best friend anymore!"

6
The Amazing Aardvark

Becky and I live on the same street, and we always bike to school together. But Monday morning she rode right by my house without stopping.

I knew she was mad at me, but I didn't think she was *that* mad. I tried to apologize all day, but she wouldn't talk to me. After school, she left without even saying good-bye!

When I got to the gym, my teammates were all in the locker room. Katie rushed right over to me.

"Dana!" she cried. "We saw you on

TV! You looked really great!"

Everyone else said nice things, too. Even Hannah Rose.

"Well, you guys were all on, too," I pointed out.

"Yeah," Amanda said. "But just for a second. You were the star!"

"Don't forget Lila!" I said. "She was the *real* star."

"You still looked great," Katie insisted. "What did Becky say about it? How was *her* party? Who — "

"Becky didn't say anything," I broke in. I felt like crying. "She isn't even talking to me. Her party was over by the time I got there. I missed the whole thing. She said I ruined her birthday."

My friends all stared at me with wide eyes.

"Poor Becky!" Katie groaned. "Poor you!"

"I know," I said with a sniffle. "Becky

and I had a huge fight. She doesn't want to be my best friend anymore."

"That's not fair," Amanda chimed in. "It's not as if you missed her party on purpose. Doesn't Becky know how important the Nationals are? I think she's being really mean and selfish."

"Me, too," Hannah Rose agreed.

"Oh, no," Katie said. "Becky isn't like that. She probably just got her feelings hurt. I'm sure she'll forgive you soon."

"I hope so," I whispered.

"In the meantime, Dana, you still have us!" Katie told me. My teammates all nodded.

"Thanks," I said. "You're good friends."

"Do you feel better now?" Katie asked.

"Uh-huh," I said. But I didn't really. A good friend is one thing. A *best* friend is another! Besides, I didn't blame Becky for being mad. I had been a terrible friend.

"Well, I think you should forget about Becky's party," Amanda told me. "There's nothing you can do about it now."

"That's right," Katie said. "And your party is this weekend! It will be so much fun! Your mom always gets such yummy cakes, and you make those great piñatas."

"Yeah," I said. "But Becky and I always make the piñatas together. This time I'll have to do it by myself."

"No, you won't," Katie promised. "Amanda and I will help you. That's what friends are for. Right, Amanda?

"Sure," Amanda said. "We can do it tomorrow."

On Tuesday, Becky still wouldn't talk to me. But at least my mom wasn't mad anymore.

Katie and Amanda came over right after school. I had already spread the piñata stuff out on the kitchen table. There was a stack of old newspapers, a bowl of flour-and-water paste, a bunch of balloons, and some masking tape.

"What kind of animal do you think we should make?" I asked Katie.

"How about a dog?" she said. Katie is crazy about dogs.

"Becky and I did a dog last year," I told her. "Remember?"

"I forgot," Katie said. "What about a cat?"

"Uh-uh," I said. "We did that three years ago."

"Did you ever have a horse?" Amanda spoke up.

"Nope," I said.

"All *riiight*!" Katie and Amanda yelled together.

"Now what?" Amanda said as we sat down at the table.

"Now we tear the paper into strips," I explained.

"How big?" Katie asked.

I tried to remember what size strips Becky and I always used, but I wasn't sure. "I don't think it matters," I said.

Soon there was a big pile of shredded newspaper on the table. "What do we do with this?" Amanda asked.

"Nothing yet," I replied. "First we have to blow up the balloons. The round ones are for the head and body, and the long skinny ones are for the legs. Then we tape them together so they look like a horse."

"That sounds easy," Katie said. It wasn't, though. The balloons wouldn't stay still. They kept floating away. But we finally got them taped.

"Now comes the *really* easy part," I said. "You have to dip the newspaper into the paste so it gets real gloppy. Then you stick it all over the balloons."

It took a long time to cover the balloons. By the time we were done, the whole kitchen was a mess. So were we.

I looked at Katie and burst out laughing. One of her pigtails had fallen into the paste and was stiff as a board. Amanda bent the pigtail in half and it made a cracking sound. Then Amanda and Katie started laughing, too.

For a minute I forgot all about the piñata. But when I took a good look at it, I stopped laughing. It didn't look anything like a horse. It didn't even look like a piñata! It looked like a big lump of mushy paper.

"Oh, no!" I cried. "Look what we did!"

Katie and Amanda looked at the piñata. They stopped laughing, too.

"I thought you knew how to do this," Amanda said to me.

"I thought so, too," I answered.

"I don't get it, Dana," Katie said. "Your piñatas always looked so beautiful before."

I poked at the blob on the table. I couldn't figure out what went wrong.

"I guess Becky must have done most of the piñata-making," I said after a while. "I mostly did the candy-stuffing."

"Well, I'm sure our piñata will look better when it's painted," Katie said. She never likes to say anything bad.

"No, it won't!" I moaned. "This is the ugliest thing I've ever seen. No one will know it's a horse!"

Amanda picked up the piñata and turned it around in her hands. "Dana's right," she declared. "This nose is way too big for a horse! And how come it has five legs?"

"That's not a leg — it's a tail!" Katie protested.

"Are you sure?" Amanda asked. "It looks like a leg to me."

"Well, it isn't!" Katie said, snatching the piñata out of Amanda's hands. She pulled off half of the tail, smooshed it up, and stuck it onto the horse's nose.

"Katie!" I cried. "What are you doing? You're making it worse!"

"No, I'm not," Katie said. "I'm making it an aardvark!"

"A what?" Amanda demanded.

"An aardvark," Katie repeated. "It's an anteater. It has a long, long nose that it sticks down anthills to suck up ants."

"Yuck!" I said. "That's gross!"

"No, it's not," Katie said. "It's amazing." Katie thinks all animals are amazing. She's going to be a veterinarian or a zookeeper when she grows up.

Katie went over to my encyclopedias and pulled down the *A* book. "Here," she said, pointing to a picture of an ugly little animal with a long, pointy nose. "See for yourself."

"Yuck!" I said again. "It looks like a big rat."

"I think it looks very intelligent," Katie said.

"*I* think it looks just like our piñata!" Amanda said.

Katie looked from the picture to the piñata. "Oh, my gosh! It does!" she shrieked. And she began to laugh again. So did Amanda.

But I didn't see what was so funny. When Becky and I made the piñatas, they always came out perfect.

When she finally stopped laughing, Katie got up from the table. "We'd better go now," she said. "It's getting late."

"But what about my piñata?" I cried.

"Don't worry, Dana," Katie said. "It

isn't finished yet. We'll come back tomorrow and help you paint it."

"Never mind," I said. "I can do *that* part myself."

On the way out, Katie patted the aardvark's head. " 'Bye, Dana," she said. "See you tomorrow."

Amanda patted the aardvark, too. But she didn't say good-bye. She was laughing too hard.

After my friends left, Mom and Woof came into the kitchen. Woof took one look at the piñata and started to growl. Then she put her tail between her legs and crept under the table.

My mother didn't say anything at first. She just stared at the piñata. "That's a nice . . . elephant," she finally said.

"It's not supposed to be an elephant!" I cried. "It's supposed to be an aardvark!"

Mom gave the piñata another look.

Then she squeezed my shoulder. "Maybe you should call Becky," she suggested. "I bet she could fix this up in no time."

Suddenly I felt like crying. "How can you call someone who isn't speaking to you?" I asked, blinking back the tears.

But I already knew the answer.

You can't!

7
My Becky-less Birthday

Early Sunday morning, Freddy jumped on my bed and started bouncing up and down. "Wake up, Dana!" he yelled. "Wake up! It's your birthday!"

I opened one eye, and Woof climbed on the bed, too.

"So how does it feel to be ten?" my dad's voice boomed from the doorway.

I pulled the covers over my head. "Sleepy," I said. "What time is it?"

Freddy pulled the covers off. "It's pancake time!"

"Well, why didn't you say so!" I

laughed. I hopped out of bed, grabbed my robe, and ran downstairs.

Mom's pancakes are always worth getting up for. But they're super-special on birthdays. Every year she makes a new kind. This year's were the best. Peanut-butter chocolate-chip!

After breakfast I got ready for my party. I put on my best leotard and packed my gym bag with streamers and balloons. I put the piñata in a big shopping bag so it wouldn't get squashed.

"Ready to go?" Mom asked when I came downstairs.

I nodded. Mom was going to drop me off at Jody's Gym before she went to the bakery to pick up my cake.

"Katie and Amanda said they would meet me at the gym," I told her. "They're going to help me decorate."

"What about . . . ?" Mom's voice trailed off. I knew she was going to ask about Becky, but I'm glad she didn't. I felt bad enough already. How could I have a birthday without my best friend?

"I told you it would look better after you painted it," Katie said when I showed her the pink-and-green piñata.

"It doesn't look better," I replied. "Just brighter."

"Well, don't feel bad," Katie said. "The candy will still taste good. And the decorations are great."

I looked around the gym. We had taped about a million balloons to the walls and covered all the equipment with crepe paper. A big HAPPY BIRTHDAY sign was hanging on top of the doorway. Katie made that — and Coach Jody's assistant, Buddy, had helped us put it up.

"It looks okay," I said.

"So who else is coming?" Katie asked

as she stuck the last two balloons on the balance beam.

"Mom said I could have ten people — one for each year," I said. "So I invited you and Amanda, Hannah Rose, Liz, Emily, Georgia and Molly from the Level Six team, Coach Jody, Lila Hanks . . . and Becky."

"Lila Hanks is coming!" Katie cried.

"Just for a while," I said. "She has ballet this afternoon, but she's going to stop by after." Even though Lila is much older than us, she's very friendly. She and Katie are Tumbling Buddies. That means they work out together once a week.

"Then I get to say good-bye to her *again*!" Katie said happily.

"Do you think Becky will come?" Amanda asked.

"I don't know," I said. "I put an invitation in her mailbox yesterday, but she still isn't talking to me."

"Well, she *should* come," Katie said. "It's going to be a great party."

The party was supposed to start at 1:30, but Coach Jody came fifteen minutes early. We had just finished hanging the aardvark from the top of the uneven parallel bars.

Coach Jody smiled when she saw our decorations. "Am I in the right gym?" she asked. "This place looks fantastic!"

"Do you really like it?" I asked.

"I love it!" Coach Jody said. "Happy birthday, kiddo!"

A few minutes later my parents and Freddy walked in with the cake. Molly and Georgia came next, and Emily, Liz, and Hannah Rose were right behind them.

At exactly 1:30, Katie cried, "It's time to start the party! Let's break the piñata!"

"Not yet," I said. "I don't want to do it till Lila gets here." But the person I was really waiting for was Becky.

For the next hour we played tumbling games, and Coach Jody showed us some great new tricks. But I kept looking over at the door. I couldn't help hoping Becky would show up — even though I knew she probably wouldn't.

When we got tired of tumbling, Mom brought out a special game she made for the party. It was just like Pin the Tail on the Donkey, except you had to pin a little gymnast onto a balance beam.

At 2:30 the door to the gym opened. I held my breath, hoping it would be Becky. But it was Lila Hanks.

"Who wants cake?" my mother asked a few minutes later.

"I do!" Freddy yelled.

"Can't we wait a little longer?" I asked. "Maybe Becky will still come."

"Sure," Mom said. "Why don't you all play one more game to really work up an appetite?" So we played Musical Mats until we dropped. That's Musical Chairs, but without the chairs.

Finally, Mom came over and whispered in my ear. "It's almost three-thirty, honey. I think we should serve the cake now."

"I guess," I said. There was no point in waiting any longer. I had to admit it: Becky really wasn't coming to my birthday party. We really weren't best friends anymore.

Everybody went *"Ooh!"* when my mom and dad brought out the cake. It had thick, gooey chocolate all around the sides and a picture of a gymnast in red, white, and blue icing on top. *HAPPY BIRTHDAY DANA* was written across it in fancy yellow writing.

The *DANA* part was all smudged.

I looked at Freddy. "I didn't do it!" he said, popping a sticky yellow finger into his mouth.

Mom lit the candles. There were ten

white ones plus a red one for good luck. Then everyone sang "Happy Birthday" to me.

"Now make a wish and blow out the candles," Dad said.

I looked around at my friends and family. They were all smiling at me. But suddenly I felt like crying. For the first time in my whole life, I was going to blow out the candles alone.

I looked down at my cake. Now I knew how Becky felt when I didn't come to *her* party.

"Make a wish, honey," Mom said.

At least I knew what to wish for. There was only one thing I really wanted. I closed my eyes and wished that Becky and I would be best friends again — best friends forever.

I blew on the candles with all my might — it was hard without Becky to help me.

When the cake was gone, we broke the

piñata. Then it was time for the presents.

I got a great gymnastics video, a bright green leotard, fuzzy gray mittens with cat faces on them, a 1,000-piece jigsaw puzzle, and lots of other stuff.

The best present was from Katie — a pogo stick! And the funniest was seven pairs of underpants with the days of the week embroidered on the back. I didn't even have to read the card to guess who they were from. They were *so* Amanda!

I said thank you to all my friends. They said happy birthday to me. And that was the end of the party.

After everyone else went home, Dad carried all the boxes out to our car. I got to sit up front with my mother because it was my birthday. Freddy and my dad had to sit in the back.

"Well, that was fun," Mom said as we drove away from the gym. "Everyone seemed to have a wonderful time."

Everyone except me, I thought. But I didn't say anything. I didn't want my parents to feel bad. Besides, I was afraid I might cry if I tried to talk.

I wished this was last Sunday instead of this Sunday. If I could do things over, I wouldn't miss Becky's party — even if I never got to be on TV! But it was too late.

I had already lost my very best friend in the world.

As we drove past Becky's house, I stared at her front door. I wondered if she was home. I wondered if she missed me as much as I missed her.

I'm going to find out, I decided. I never want to have another birthday without my best friend!

The minute the car pulled into our driveway, I opened the door and jumped out. "I'll be back soon," I told my parents.

Then I ran down the street to Becky's house.

Best Friends Forever

I stood outside the Berkmans' door and took a deep breath. Maybe this wasn't such a good idea. What if Becky wouldn't talk to me? What if she wouldn't even let me in?

There was only one way to find out. I rang the bell.

Becky opened the door. She looked surprised to see me. But I couldn't tell if she was surprised mad or surprised glad.

"Hi, Beck," I said.

"Hi," she answered.

"Can I come in?" I asked.

"I guess," Becky said.

I followed her into the kitchen. For a minute we just stood there, staring at each other.

"Well?" Becky said.

Now that I was here, I wasn't sure what to say. I looked at the refrigerator door. A bunch of birthday cards were stuck to it with magnets.

"I never wished you a happy birthday," I finally said.

"I know," Becky said. "I didn't wish you one either."

There was another long silence. Then we both said "Happy birthday!" at exactly the same time.

"So . . . how was your party?" Becky asked.

"It was okay," I said. "All the girls on my team were there, plus Coach Jody, and my family, and some of the Level Six girls. Even Lila Hanks came."

"Wow!" Becky said. "A real National Gymnast came to your party."

"Well, just for a little while," I said. "She showed Freddy how to use the mini trampoline. He spent the whole party bouncing up and down like a maniac."

"Did he throw up?" Becky asked. Freddy does that a lot.

"Not this time," I said. "Which is really a miracle. Because my mom got me this humongous cake with red, white, and blue icing, and Freddy ate the whole top."

There was another long silence.

"Was your party fun?" Becky asked.

"Not really," I admitted. "Nothing is fun without you, Becky."

"I know," Becky said. "My party wasn't any good, either."

For a minute neither of us said anything. Then, for the second time in five minutes, we both said the exact same thing at the exact same time:

"I should have gone to your party!"

We both laughed. Then we gave each other big birthday hugs.

"You're way more important than Lila Hanks, or gymnastics, or anything," I said. "I'm sorry I made you feel bad."

"And I'm sorry I said you weren't my best friend anymore," Becky said. "If there was a big karate exhibition, with TV cameras and everything, I probably would have wanted to go, too. But that wouldn't mean karate is more important than you are."

"I guess," I said. "But I think I liked it better when we were little and we used to do everything together. I wish it could still be like that."

"Then you would have had to quit gymnastics when I did," Becky pointed out. "And I couldn't have taken karate lessons or juggling lessons, or tap-dancing lessons, or trumpet les — "

"All right! All right! I get the point!" I giggled.

"My mom said that the older we get, the more different we'll become," Becky said. "But I hope we don't become too different."

"Let's make a promise," I said. "Even if we never want to do the same things, we'll always be best friends."

"Definitely," Becky said. "And we'll always blow out our birthday candles together. Even when we're a hundred years old!"

"Definitely," I agreed. "Best friends forever!"

We high-fived.

"I have an idea," I said. "Do you have any cupcakes or Twinkies?"

"Are you kidding?" Becky grinned.

"Sorry!" I said. "I forgot where I was for a minute." Becky's dad is a total health nut. Practically all the Berkmans ever eat is fruit and veggies. They *never* have sweets in their house.

"How about a bran muffin?" I asked. "Or a seven-grain roll?"

"That's more like it," Becky said. "Help yourself."

I opened the cupboard and began pulling stuff out. There was a giant box of wheat crackers, an unsliced loaf of zucchini bread, and a package of fat-free, sugarless prune tarts.

"Yuck!" I said. "Is this all you have?"

Becky bit into a prune tart and made a face. "What are you looking for?" she asked.

"Wait a minute," I said. "I think I found it." I held up a pumpernickel-raisin bagel.

There were two red candles on the table. I pulled one out of its silver candle-holder and stuck it in the bagel hole. It fit perfectly!

"What do you think?" I asked.

Becky looked at my homemade birthday cake and burst out laughing. Without a word, she took a matchbook off the kitchen counter and lit the fat red candle.

"Happy birthday to you . . ." I began to sing.

"Happy birthday to you . . ." Becky sang.

"Happy birthday to uh-ussss!" we sang together.

"Happy birthday to us!"

Then, we both leaned over and closed our eyes. Together, my best friend and I blew out our birthday candle.